I am Maria

by Toby Talbot / illustrated by Eleanor Mill

COWLES BOOK COMPANY, INC.
NEW YORK

Text copyright 1969 by Toby Talbot

Illustrations copyright 1969 by Eleanor Mill

SBN 402-14031-1

Library of Congress Catalog Card Number 72-87084

Cowles Book Company, Inc.
A subsidiary of Cowles Communications , Inc.

Published simultaneously in Canada by
General Publishing Company, Ltd.,
30 Lesmill Road, Don Mills, Toronto, Ontario

Printed in the United States of America

First Edition

I am Maria

María sat at the window looking out. It was a strange, lonely world outside and she did not want to join it. She had arrived in New York from the Dominican Republic only last month. The English words she heard seemed harsh and ugly to her ears. They were words she never cared to learn. She dreaded September, when school would begin and she would have to learn or else seem stupid. Imagine a nine-year-old who couldn't speak English!

Inside was María's world — the friendly sounds of Spanish, the spicy smell of thick black beans simmering on the stove, the presence of her mother with skin the color of coffee and milk, black sad eyes, and gold earrings that danced from her ears even when she scolded.

"Once I was happy," María whispered to herself. "Here I am lost. I don't feel like me."

In Santo Domingo her family had lived in a straw hut near the sea. There she went barefoot. Her father worked in the fields and came home for lunch and siesta. The whole *barrio,* their neighborhood, smelled deliciously of garlic and olive oil. Every afternoon she would have a snack of bread with a chunk of chocolate. When they left, her mother's eyes had filled with big tears. When María asked her father why they had to leave, his answer was, "Here it is poor. *Así es la vida* ['such is life']."

Now, when she looked out the window, María saw only hard pavement, which meant she had to wear shoes all the time. Father was at work all day long, and whenever Mother got letters from home, the same big tears filled her eyes.

María sighed. She went over to the cupboard and poured a little olive oil into a dish and began dunking bits of bread and eating them. Whenever she was homesick, that's what she did.

"María," her mother called.

Her mother was at the ironing board and smelled like sunshine and fresh laundry.

6

"Please go down to the *bodega* and buy three *plátanos* and a bread."

"Must I, Mamá?" María asked.

"*Por favor,* we need them for lunch," her mother said.

María did not like the thought of going out. But at least they spoke Spanish at the *bodega*. She decided to take her doll, Dolores, for company.

As she stood in the hall she heard a baby crying on the floor above. She went down one flight of steps. A radio was blaring a commercial — "*Pepsi-Cola refresca más . . .*" Down on the next floor María saw an open door. Inside at a sewing machine sat an old woman with white hair and blue eyes. The machine was whirring away and seemed to be gobbling up the dress that the woman was sewing. Near the woman stood a dressmaker's dummy in a white satin dress with silver beads sewn at the neck. And all around the room were beautiful scraps of red and purple and yellow fabric, gauzy like butterflies.

María stopped and stared. The woman seemed like the queen of a glorious rag pile. Maybe she's a dressmaker, thought María. In the Dominican Republic one of their

neighbors had a sewing machine on which she stitched clothes. But this woman was sitting in a wheelchair as she sewed. That was strange.

The woman must have felt María staring at her, for she looked up and her blue eyes smiled. María felt like a snooper and hurried down the last flight of steps.

"Why does she keep her door open?" María thought. "Someday somebody's going to kidnap her and it will serve her right. But who ever heard of kidnapping an old lady?"

As she considered this, María walked down the stoop, climbing over their neighbor, José, who was tuning his guitar. As she passed, José broke into a familiar song. It was a song about a man cutting sugarcane in the fields and telling his love all the things he would bring her when he returned. María sighed. She was sighing a lot these days.

"*Hola, muñeca,*" José said when he finished his song. *Muñeca* meant "doll," but María knew that he was talking to her and not to Dolores.

"*Buenos días,* José. Who's the lady in the wheelchair?"

"Oh, the dressmaker? She can't walk. She just stays in her room all day long and sews. People come and bring her fabric and she makes them dresses. They also bring her food and things."

"*Hasta luego,* José," María said as she went on her way.

"*Adiós, niña,*" he called after her. Then he struck up a mournful tune about a man who tells his love that he wants to marry her, but is so poor he can provide her only with bread and onions. "*Contigo pan y cebollas,*" he wailed.

María had to cross Broadway to reach the *bodega*. She hated that street. Everything looked gray. The wind blew sharp and dusty, and the cars flew by as if they would not stop until they reached the sea. She missed the first green light because the traffic made her dizzy. When she was half-way across, she reached an island of benches, but then the light suddenly turned to red and she had to wait again. An old man was sitting on a bench eating a roll, and he looked pale and sad. María wondered why everyone in New York looked unhappy. His eyes met hers for a moment, but she quickly dropped hers and would not speak to him in eye language. She wanted nothing to do with the New York world.

The light changed and she crossed. When she looked back the man was staring straight ahead.

12

María walked halfway down the street to the *bodega*. As soon as she entered, everything smelled good — the roasted coffee, black olives, and familiar cheeses. A customer's conversation with the owner in fast Spanish sounded like a song to her. The counter was filled with beans and more beans: plump red kidney beans, white *garbanzos*, round little black beans, gray lentils, and impish black-eyed beans that seemed to be winking at you. Strings of garlic and *chorizo* sausages hung behind the counter.

"Tres plátanos y un pan," said María, ordering her plantains and bread.

As she left the store a moment later with her purchases, she saw a man wearing sandwich boards. He was handing out leaflets. On the boards she read the advertisement: "MADAME ZORINA TELLS YOUR FORTUNE — in Spanish and English." Before María knew it, the man had handed her a leaflet printed in both languages and was on his way. She read the Spanish: "Madame Zorina removes bad luck. She lifts you out of sorrow and darkness and starts you on the way to happiness. See her today. Tomorrow may be too late."

"Who needs this?" María said to herself. "I know my fortune — misery."

As she was looking at the leaflet, a man bumped into her and banged her nose. He mumbled something in English and hurried on. María's nose hurt. She felt like crying.

"I'm going home and never leave the house again," she decided. "The only thing outside your door is trouble."

She crossed the street. The same old man was sitting on the same old bench. Once again their eyes met. This time he smiled. Without thinking, María smiled back at him. Her eyes had recognized him and smiled on their own.

The leaflet was still in her hand. "Maybe I ought to go to Madame Zorina," she thought. "I might as well know the worst."

Madame Zorina, it turned out, was only two blocks away. She was a gypsy and looked like a bright-feathered bird. She wore a red skirt, a yellow blouse, and a flowered scarf on her head. Two gold teeth glimmered from the upper left corner of her mouth. When she opened the door, which was hung with brass cowbells, she seemed not at all surprised to see María.

"How much do you have?" she asked in Spanish.

María looked down at the money in her hand. Her grocery change was twenty-five cents. She showed it to the fortune-teller.

The woman grabbed it and, again in Spanish, said, "It will be a *rápido*." María understood that to mean she would get a fast reading.

The gypsy pulled María over to a chair in front of which was a crystal ball.

"Crystal ball or palm?" she asked.

"Palm," answered María, not sure what the gypsy might do with the crystal ball.

Madame Zorina studied María's palm and traced the lines on it. It tickled, but María felt too uneasy to laugh. She clutched her doll tighter.

"You are going to meet a stranger," the woman told her.

"What is . . . ?" María was about to ask who.

The woman paid no attention and went on. "There is a great danger lying ahead of you. But the stranger will save you from it. You must take great care and follow your heart's bidding. *Terminado,*" she announced abruptly. The reading was finished.

Before María knew it, Madame Zorina had shoved her out the door and she was once again in the street. The growls in her stomach and the thought of the green *plátanos* that her mother would fry into crispy *tostones* quickened her steps toward home.

When she got to her house, her eyes traveled upward, hoping to see her mother at the window. For often when María went on an errand her mother would watch for her

return. But nothing was in her window except a flapping shade. As her eyes moved downward, though, they caught sight of the dressmaker sitting at her window. The woman was beckoning with her hands. María thought she was calling to someone else and turned to see who was behind her. No one was there except some men on a truck collecting garbage.

María tried to think how she could sneak past the dressmaker's apartment without facing her. Oh, she didn't want to get mixed up with strangers, especially blue-eyed, English-speaking ones!

But, how unlucky! When María reached the first floor landing, that same door was open and the woman had wheeled her chair to the doorway.

Again the dressmaker was smiling. María thought it was funny that she smiled without demanding a return smile. A bundle wrapped in muslin lay on her lap. As soon as María appeared she held it out. María shook her head.

The woman nodded just as insistently, pointed to María's doll, and pressed the bundle on her. María grabbed

it and ran. As she escaped up the stairs she heard the woman's voice calling after her, "I am Mrs. Bailey."

"Why do you delay?" her mother scolded when she dashed through the door. Without waiting to hear María's excuse, she took the package of groceries and disappeared into the kitchen. Soon María heard the music of sizzling olive oil.

She opened the bundle. Inside was a beautiful jumble of scraps — pale blue silk, velvet as black as a crow's wing, satin as orange as a mango, and snips of gilt ribbon. As María fingered the cloth, the parting words, "I am Mrs. Bailey," ran through her head. She knew that "Mrs." meant "*Señora.*" Mrs. Bailey must be the name of the dressmaker.

María at once set to making clothes for Dolores. By evening the doll was decked out as grandly as a princess. "*Muñeca,* you look so gay," María crooned.

That evening her mother sent her out to buy more bread, a head of garlic, some parsley, and a pound of tomatoes. The crybaby upstairs was laughing now and the radio downstairs was playing a *cha-cha-cha.* As María descended

the next flight she held her breath, planning to sneak past the dressmaker's open door. But life, as they say, is full of surprises. The dressmaker's door was shut.

"Oh, why is she like that?" María complained under her breath. "Opening and shutting her door all day long?" She began walking down the steps, when suddenly the fortune-teller's words hummed in her ears — "A stranger . . . you must follow your heart's bidding."

María followed her heart. It told her to turn back. She walked straight to the door and knocked. At first there was no answer. Getting braver as she stood there, she knocked again, louder.

"Come in," a feeble voice answered. "Come in" was babble to María's ears, but the sound of the voice meant *entre*. María turned the knob and let herself in.

Mrs. Bailey had fallen off her wheelchair, which had rolled out of reach. She was pale and breathing hard, like someone who has run a long distance and is very tired. She did not say anything, but her eyes looked deeply into María's. For a moment María felt like running away. What was she

doing here with this stranger? She should be going to the *bodega*. There everyone spoke her language.

But somehow she couldn't leave. The woman needed her. The eyes were still fixed upon hers.

María ran over and pushed the wheelchair close to Mrs. Bailey. Then she placed the woman's arms around her own shoulders for support. As Mrs. Bailey leaned heavily on her, María, with great effort, slowly raised her back into the wheelchair.

Exhausted and damp with perspiration, Mrs. Bailey looked at María gratefully. Neither of them spoke. Now María had no desire to leave and the woman's eyes said, "Stay."

After a while Mrs. Bailey began to look rosier and was breathing in a more normal way. Soon she looked at María and smiled, but did not speak. She was still too weak.

The girl looked into the old woman's eyes. A warm, friendly feeling flooded María and her face tingled. This stranger was no longer strange. Nor was the place. She was not lost, but at home, in a new home.

She looked into the woman's eyes, smiled back, and her first English words were born:
"I am María."